John Burningham

Motor Miles

JONATHAN CAPE • LONDON

Miles, our
much-loved
difficult dog.

Some other picture books by John Burningham

Picnic	Mr Gumpy's Motor Car	Husherbye
Borka	Mr Gumpy's Outing	Granpa
Tug of War	Avocado Baby	Courtney
Simp	The Magic Bed	Humbert
Aldo	Whadayamean	Cloudland
Where's Julius	Oi! Get Off Our Train	The Shopping Basket
Come Away From the Water, Shirley	Edwardo, the Horriblest Boy in the Whole Wide World	Time to Get Out of the Bath, Shirley
	John Patrick Norman McHennessy	
	Would You Rather?	

JONATHAN CAPE

UK | USA | Canada | Ireland | Australia
India | New Zealand | South Africa

Jonathan Cape is part of the Penguin Random House group of companies
whose addresses can be found at global.penguinrandomhouse.com.

www.penguin.co.uk   www.puffin.co.uk   www.ladybird.co.uk

Penguin
Random House
UK

First published 2016
001

Copyright © John Burningham, 2016
The moral right of the author has been asserted

Printed in China
CIP catalogue record for this book is available from the British Library

ISBN: 978-0-857-55174-0

All correspondence to:
Jonathan Cape, Penguin Random House Children's,
80 Strand, London WC2R 0RL

MIX
Paper from
responsible sources
FSC® C018179

This is Miles.
Miles was given a home by Alice Trudge
and her son, Norman.
But Miles was a very difficult dog.

Miles did not come when he was called,

did not like going for walks,

did not like his food.

Or the rain.

He barked too much

and he didn't like other dogs.

Alice Trudge and Norman were very fond
of Miles even though he was difficult.

What Miles really liked was to go out
in the car and up the hill to the café,

where people said,
"Oh, what a lovely dog."

"I can't go on day after day taking the dog out in the car just to please him," said Alice Trudge.

"What your dog needs is his own car,"
said Mr Huddy, the man who lived next door.

"How can I possibly get a car for the dog?"
said Alice Trudge.

"I will make a car for Miles," said Mr Huddy.

So Mr Huddy started to make the car
for Miles. And every day after school,
Miles and Norman used to go and see
the car being made.

Finally, Mr Huddy had finished the car and it was ready for Miles.

"We will have to get you driving lessons," said Mr Huddy to Miles.

Going right,

going left,

going backwards.

Quick STOP!

After many lessons, Miles had learned to drive and was ready to go on the road.

One morning Alice Trudge could not
take Norman to school and did not know
what to do.

"I could squeeze into Miles's car and he
could take me to school," said Norman.

When Norman arrived at school in a car driven by a dog, all the other children were amazed.

And Norman and Miles even used to go for secret little trips in the car.

One day they went to the seaside very early
in the morning.

Other mornings they would drive out into
the countryside,

through leaves in the autumn,

and once, in the winter, they drove out
and played in the snow.

Miles was getting easier.

He liked walks,

 his food,

other dogs,

didn't mind the rain,

barked less

and came when he was called.

Norman was growing up and getting bigger and soon he could no longer fit in the car.

Miles stopped driving; maybe he didn't like being on his own. So the car was put away.

One day Miles and Norman heard a lot of
noise coming from Mr Huddy's workshop.

"Let's go and see what Huddy is up to now,"
said Norman.

Mr Huddy was starting to make an aeroplane.

I wonder who that is for?